DISNEY

THE
LION KING

Miss Doig says
excellent work

Ladybird

As a new day began on the African plain, the sun rose on an amazing sight. Cheetahs, elephants, giraffes – animals and birds of every kind – were hurrying towards Pride Rock. They were gathering to welcome Simba, the newborn son of Mufasa, the Lion King, and Queen Sarabi.

As the vast crowd waited, Rafiki, a mystic, ancient baboon, approached Mufasa and Sarabi. He gave the new cub his blessing. Carrying him carefully to the edge of Pride Rock, Rafiki held Simba high above the throng.

"There he is!" the animals all shouted, bursting into cheers. "Welcome! Welcome Prince Simba!"

After the ceremony King Mufasa and his adviser, Zazu, went to find Scar, the King's younger brother. "Sarabi and I were disappointed not to see you at Simba's presentation this morning," Mufasa said to him.

Scar looked straight ahead. He wasn't interested in the celebration – all he cared about was becoming king himself, and the arrival of Simba had spoiled his chances! "Sorry, it must have slipped my mind," he said, as he began to walk away.

Mufasa's deep voice stopped him. "Don't turn your back on me, Scar!"

Scar spun round. "Perhaps *you* shouldn't turn your back on *me*, Mufasa," he growled.

"Are you threatening me?" the King demanded.

Scar didn't answer, but stalked away defiantly.

Simba was a happy, lively cub. He loved exploring the Pride Lands with his father or with Nala, a lioness cub who was his best friend. There was only one place forbidden to him – the shadowy land beyond the northern border. It was so dangerous that Mufasa would not even tell Simba what was out there.

But Simba's devious Uncle Scar was keen to tell him. "It's an elephant graveyard," said Scar, "and only the *bravest* lions can venture into it. That's why you *mustn't* go there."

But I am brave, thought Simba, *and I'll prove it to Father!*

One day, as Zazu was keeping an eye on the youngsters, Simba urged Nala to follow him as quickly as she could so that they could lose Zazu.

"Where are we going?" asked Nala, giggling.

"To an elephant graveyard," Simba told her. "Come on, hurry!"

By the time Zazu caught up with the cubs, they had reached the forbidden land – the elephant graveyard.

"You must leave here immediately!" he squawked. "We're all in great danger!"

Suddenly three giggling, drooling hyenas emerged from an elephant skull. Baring their fangs, they surrounded Zazu and the cubs.

Desperately trying to be brave, Simba tried to roar – but all he could manage was a squeaky rumble. The hyenas laughed and moved in closer.

All at once a huge *ROAAARRR!* split the air. The hyenas whirled round and looked straight into the eyes of Mufasa.

"It's the King!" shouted a hyena called Shenzi. "Let's get out of here!"

Later when they were alone, Mufasa told Simba, "I'm disappointed in you, son. You disobeyed me and you put Nala and Zazu in danger."

"I'm sorry, Father," said Simba. "I was just trying to be brave like you."

"Being brave doesn't mean you go looking for trouble," Mufasa explained. Simba hung his head in shame.

"Look up at the stars, son," said Mufasa, more gently. "The great kings of the past gaze down at us from those stars. They are part of the great Circle of Life and they will always be there to guide you – and so will I. Remember that."

"I'll remember," Simba promised.

Meanwhile Scar was scowling down at the three hyenas.
"You idiots!" he hissed. "You had the perfect
opportunity to kill Simba – and Mufasa."

The hyenas couldn't believe what they'd heard. "Why
should we kill Mufasa?" asked Shenzi.

"Because with *both* of them gone, *I* would
become the new King!" replied Scar.
"So, stick with me and I'll make
sure you're treated well."

"Sounds good to me," said the
hyena called Banzai.

"Then listen," said Scar. "I have
a plan."

As they listened,
Shenzi and Banzai
grinned and Ed
laughed menacingly.

The next day, while Mufasa took his daily walk along the cliffs, Scar ordered the hyenas to start a stampede, and he lured Simba into the trap he had set for him.

"Mufasa!" Scar shouted, looking down at the young cub, who was clinging, terrified, to a branch. "The wildebeest are stampeding. Simba's in danger!"

"I'm coming!" Mufasa shouted, leaping down to rescue his son. He grabbed Simba and swiftly carried him to safety.

But as he tried to climb back up onto the cliffs, Mufasa fell backwards. Clinging to an overhanging rock, he gasped to his brother, "Scar, help me!"

"Long live the King!" sneered Scar, and seizing his chance, he pushed Mufasa down to his death.

Simba rushed to his father's lifeless body and began to cry.

"This is all *your* fault," said an icy voice beside him. It was Scar! "If the King hadn't tried to save you, he'd still be alive," he lied. "You can never show your face in the Pride again. Run away – and *never* return!"

Heartbroken, Simba fled. Scar ordered Shenzi and Banzai to catch Simba and kill him.

Meanwhile Scar made his way back to the Pride and proclaimed himself the new King. He told Sarabi that her husband and son were dead. But what he didn't know was that the hyenas had failed to catch Simba – he was still alive!

Hot, thirsty and exhausted, Simba staggered on until, unable to go any further, he fainted.

When Simba woke up, a skinny meerkat, called Timon, was pouring water into his mouth while a fat warthog, named Pumbaa, looked on.

"You nearly died," Pumbaa told Simba. "We saved you."

"Thanks," said Simba, "but you shouldn't have bothered. It doesn't matter whether I live or die."

"That sounds serious," said Timon. "Put your troubles behind you and live in the jungle with us. *Hakuna matata* – no worries! That's what we say!"

Simba thought for a moment. "All right," he agreed.

"Good!" exclaimed Timon. "Now for something to eat!" He ran off and returned with a selection of fat, slimy bugs. Simba turned away in disgust but he was so hungry he finally tried one. He was surprised at how good they tasted!

One day, many years later, Timon and Pumbaa were chased by a lioness. Hearing their cries, Simba rushed to help them – and was amazed to find that their attacker was his best friend, Nala.

Simba and Nala hugged each other joyfully. After introducing her to his friends, Simba showed Nala the jungle he had come to love.

"It's like paradise here," said Nala, "but it's not your home, Simba. Come back to Pride Rock and take your rightful place as king."

"I'm not fit to be the King," Simba said quietly. "I can never return."

"The Pride needs you," Nala persisted. "Scar has let the hyenas take over and things are terrible. Don't turn your back on your responsibilities, Simba. What would your father think?"

"My father is dead," said Simba. Blinking back tears, he turned and walked slowly away.

But Nala's words stayed with him. That night, unable to sleep, Simba went for a walk.

Rafiki, the mystic baboon, had made his way to the jungle and was waiting for Simba. It was time for Simba to take his place in the Circle of Life.

Bewildered, Simba followed Rafiki to a small, still pool.

"Look there," said the baboon, pointing at Simba's reflection in the water. Suddenly the reflection magically changed into that of Mufasa and a deep voice called from above, "*Simba!*"

"Father!" cried Simba, looking up at the clouds. Before his astonished eyes, Mufasa's image filled the sky.

"Simba, remember who you are," said the voice of Mufasa. "You are my son, and the true King. You must take your place in the Circle of Life. Remember, Simba. Remember…"

As his father's image faded, Simba knew what he had to do.

Next morning, as Nala, Timon and Pumbaa searched for Simba, Rafiki called to them from a tree.

"The King has returned to Pride Rock," he told them.

"He's gone back!" cried Nala happily, and with Pumbaa and Timon, she set out after him.

Meanwhile, as Simba neared the Pride Lands, he began to feel very sad. Drought had left the earth parched, and everywhere he looked, he saw lifeless plants and the remains of dead animals.

With his father's voice echoing in his mind, *"Remember… remember…"* Simba entered the Pride Lands. Storm clouds were gathering above him and thunder rumbled in the distance.

At Pride Rock the hyenas paced restlessly. "We're hungry," they complained, "and there's no food left!"

"It's the lionesses' job to get food," snapped Scar. "Sarabi! Where is your hunting party?"

"There is nothing left to hunt," said Sarabi. "If we don't leave Pride Rock soon we will all die."

"We're not going *anywhere!*" roared Scar.

Suddenly, a roar even louder than Scar's filled the air, and Scar saw a golden-maned lion coming towards him. He couldn't believe his eyes! He looked just like Mufasa.

Sarabi was the first to recognise her son. "Simba – you're alive," she said weakly.

"Yes," said Simba, "and I've come back to take my place as the King."

Scar quickly signalled to the starving hyenas. As they attacked, Simba stumbled and lost his foothold on the cliff edge.

Scar calmly looked down at Simba, who was desperately trying to pull himself back onto the rock.

"Now, this looks familiar," sneered Scar. "You look just like your father did before I killed him."

Simba was stunned – he wasn't responsible for his father's death, after all! Scar had murdered Mufasa!

Enraged, Simba lunged upwards, digging his claws into Scar. As they struggled, lightning struck the dry grass and smoke and flames swept over Pride Rock.

At last Scar fell to the plain below where he was killed by the angry hyenas. Simba had won the day!

As the Pride celebrated together, heavy raindrops fell around them, putting out the flames and watering the parched land.

One morning, many months later, all the birds and animals journeyed to Pride Rock to welcome another new prince – the son of King Simba and Queen Nala. As he had done many years before, Rafiki lifted the new cub high above the cheering throng.

That night Simba stood alone at the top of Pride Rock. He watched the stars begin to rise and thought about the great Circle of Life of which his own son was now a part.

"Everything's all right now, Father," Simba said, looking up at the star-filled sky. "I remembered." And one by one the stars seemed to twinkle in reply.

Ladybird books are widely available, but in case of difficulty may be ordered by post or telephone from:
Ladybird Books – Cash Sales Department Littlegate Road Paignton Devon TQ3 3BE Telephone 0803 554761

A catalogue record for this book is available from the British Library

Published by Ladybird Books Ltd Loughborough Leicestershire UK
LADYBIRD and the device of a Ladybird are trademarks of Ladybird Books Ltd